YOUR KNOWLEDGE HAS VALUE

AF167222

- We will publish your bachelor's and master's thesis, essays and papers

- Your own eBook and book - sold worldwide in all relevant shops

- Earn money with each sale

Upload your text at www.GRIN.com and publish for free

Questioning Identity in Diana Abu Jaber's book "Arabian Jazz"

Adil Ouatat

Bibliographic information published by the German National Library:

The German National Library lists this publication in the National Bibliography; detailed bibliographic data are available on the Internet at http://dnb.dnb.de.

ISBN: 9783346838810
This book is also available as an ebook.

© GRIN Publishing GmbH
Nymphenburger Straße 86
80636 München

Print and binding: Books on Demand GmbH, Norderstedt, Germany
Printed on acid-free paper from responsible sources.

The present work has been carefully prepared. Nevertheless, authors and publishers do not incur liability for the correctness of information, notes, links and advice as well as any printing errors.

GRIN web shop: https://www.grin.com/document/1334028

Dr. Adil Ouatat
High School of Training and Education
University Sultan Moulay Sliman
Béni Mellal, Morocco

Questioning Identity in Diana Abu-Jaber's Novel "*ARABIAN JAZZ*"

Abstract:
Diana Abu Jaber is one of the prominent Arab American women writers. This article aims at discussing one of the literary works of Diana Abu Jaber, namely *Arabian Jazz*, focusing on the theme of identity. In her writings, Diana Abu Jaber deploys the cultural trope to discuss the Arab-American life and issues of belonging to their homeland. Also, Diana tries to focus on the identity theme to negotiate the existence of Arab in the main stream America and how these characters suffer from the duality and how they try to preserve their homeland identity through a hybridization of both identities. In this article the focus will be on the protagonists of the novel Arabia Jazz and how Diana Abu Jaber tries to analyse the protagonists' identity in a stylistic way.
Key words: Identity, hybridity, dual identities, ethnocultural identity, Arabian Jazz, Diana Abu Jaber

1- Introduction

Arab American literature appeared at the beginning of the 1900s and began to develop through the various stages that Arabs knew in America. The social and political circumstances and events affected the Arab communities in sorting and developing this type of ethnic literature.

Most of the early Arab-American writers presented themselves as Arabs without referring to the American part of their identity, but this approach changed over time, and Arab-American writers began to take into account the space provided by the American side of their personality and began to put their experience in building identity in its multicultural American context. Instead of the literary production taking the status of Arab only or only American, writers try to create a balance between these two worlds.

The task of these writers is to make the Arab American voice heard and to confront the misperception spread about Arabs in the United States of America, and this is due to their good understanding of American society and their pride in the culture of the homeland.

This paper attempts to understand how these writers discuss the issue of identity in their writings through Diana Abu Jaber's novel *Arabian Jazz*, and it is one of post-modern novels within the Arab American literary frame.

Identity has become one of the problematic concepts in sociology for the reason that it is so fluid under the effects of globalization. According to Philip M. Khayal, "Identity formation then, is not a singular process with a definitive end point but an evolving social-psychological experience of self-discovery that changes with events, issues, and socio-political circumstances surrounding a person". In the same parallel of importance, Stuart Hall claims that the identity of diasporic people is constantly being alerted due to diasporic identity that is a fluid and transforming itself. Continuing Stuart's argument about identity, he considers identity as a "production" because identity is changeable according to the circumstances. In the long run, Homi Bhabha maintains that the change on diasporic identity and the continuity in this change lead to have a "hybrid identity"; which means the mixture of elements from the home-land and adopted home to create a third culture that reflects immigrants in diaspora to be "in betweenness". Consequently, Arab-Americans fight with similar identity politics and issues of representation that other migrants encounter.

In the Arab-American diaspora, many issues are raised to be debated over which part of this category should be focused on: Arab, American, or in between; in other words, whether a hyphen should distinguish the different elements of their ethnocultural and national identities, or if this hyphen should be replaced by a hybrid identity in which the identities are blended instead of being separated.

Identity in the Arab-American Literature is considered as one of debatable and skeptical issues because this concept; identity embodies and reflects how others build their judgments on Arabs. In this way, Robert Terwilliger argues that "a man finds his identity by identifying. A man's identity is not best thought of as the way in which he is separated from his fellows, but the way in which he is united with them." Thus, Arab-American hold a unique set of cultural values, beliefs and attitudes. They have found the conformity on keeping their culture within the dominant culture of the US.

Thus, Arab-American women's identity is presented to be in conflict. It is employed to define ethnic identity and to explain the different strategies applied by this ethnic group to adapt appropriately the new home. First and foremost, sociologists among them Atkinson, Morten and Sue have defined ethnic identities as individual's sense of belonging to a group. For those with multicultural backgrounds, the progress of ethnic identity has been conceptualized as an evolutionary stage process (1979: 23). Furthermore, ethnic identity is the community's feelings that have a linkage with values, symbols, and shared history which identify them as a distinct group.

As a result, this paper is devoted to Diana Abu Jaber's novel, *Arabian Jazz*, and analysing how Diana Abu Jaber deploys the concept of identity among Arab Americans by deconstructing the identity aspect of the main characters in the novel: Fatima, Matussem, Jemorah, and Melvina.

2-   Identity in Arab American writings

this axis will try to shed light on the treatment of the issue of identity by Arab-American writers, especially contemporaries, Diana Abu Jaber includes.

The question of identity has inspired many Arab-American writers since their early existence in the USA. And most of the writings tried to answer questions related to the issue of identity. Thus, how do contemporary writers provide answers to the question of identity? And how do some Arab American writers see the correct way to discuss it?

The first generation of Arab-American writers dealt with the question of identity differently than the current generation. Before the assimilation process reached its climax, the first generation expressed only their pure culture and their heritage through their writings, without mentioning their Americanness part. Steven Salaita (2000: 14) expresses his reservation, considering that the way they expressed their identity do not go beyond the limits of their imagination:

> *"Their task is to build a heritage identifiably linked to the Arab world but that is nonetheless their own."* [6]

This approach does not serve the Arab-Americans in their quest for integration, which made Lisa Suhair Majaj (1999: 64) calls for the adoption of a new, different approach that relies primarily on considering the Arab-American identity as an indivisible whole, celebrating both components and giving them equal importance:

> *"As hyphenated Americans we seek to integrate the different facets of ourselves, our experiences, and our heritages into a unified whole."*

In response to the hesitation of some to present their multidimensional identity and express the richness of the new multicultural environment, Majaj (1999:71) claims:

> *"As we continue to strengthen our networks and develop our group identity, we need to expand our vision and to move beyond cultural preservation toward transformation [...] We need to probe the American as well as the Arab dimensions of our Arab American identity, and to engage not only in self-assertion, but also in self-criticism."*

This new approach to identity is what the current generation of Arab-American writers has adopted. An approach formulated to reflect the cultural diversity that Arab Americans add to American society. Thus, identity and culture were invested as a kind of enrichment rather than as an element of difference.

Recently, the most important fiction writings show that Arab Americans seem ready to extrapolate the most important aspects of their identity in a way that has not been discussed before. The Arab-American writer Diana-Abu Jaber's novel *"Arabian Jazz"* is an explicit example of how Arab American writers approach the topic of hybrid identity.

3- Conceptx of identity in Diana-Abu Jaber's novel *"Arabian Jazz"*

Through the two main characters in the novel, Jemorah and Melvina, Abu Jaber discusses the question of the dual identity; in-betweenness, of Arab Americans. Throughout the novel's chapters, the older sister Jemorah (Jem) tries to find a definition of her dual identity. The conflict she is experiencing reflects Abu Jaber's analysis and investigation of the Arab-American identity. Without reaching any conclusion, Abu-Jaber deploys the jazz as a metaphor to express Jemorah's complex identity.

Like Arab culture, American society includes other dual identities, such as Latin Americans, American Indians, African Americans, etc. And all these identities struggle to prove their presence within the multicultural stream of American society. Abu Jaber referred to this topic in her writings to clarify that Arab Americans, like other minorities, have common connections represented in the struggle for identity. In this context, the relationship of Jemorah with Ricky, exemplifying this as an event through which Abu Jaber highlights that many other characters belonging to different heritage have the same issue as Arabs. Ricky, as he belongs to an Indian background, is also searching for himself through the identity conflict he is experiencing.

In this regard, Steven Salaita argues:

> " In Arabian Jazz, contextualizing the Arab within a broader rubric of minority discourse produces a textual paradox worth our attention: Abu Jaber creates an essentialized Other—the Arab American— who interacts with other marginalized characters so that the essentialist tendencies of the dominant society can be mitigated and ultimately restructured." (2001:436)

Abu Jaber chooses a small, poor white town called Euclid, where the novel takes place, and as an environment for the main characters to explore the complexity of their identities through their interaction with the place. Here, Abu Jaber wants to point out that the town is marginalized by society, just as the Arab family is. Salaita states, "It is in the community where critics can see living contrasts of preservation and assimilation, Arabism and Americana, xenophobia and camaraderie - all split visions that demand expressions." (2000)

By setting the events of the novel in an isolated town, Abu-Jaber aims to draw attention to how this small community perceives values and how it understands differences.

The place has a strong connotation in the novel, and the town of Euclid became home to an Arab family in America, the Matussem Ramoud family, and his two daughters, Jemorah and Melvina.

> "Without the mall, Euclid remained an amoeba of a town, thirty miles straight out Route 31 north of Syracuse. It took in dirt farmers, onion farmers, and junk dealers and produced poorly clothed and poorly fed children, who'd wait for driver's licenses then leave in rotting-out Chevies, going as far as a case of Black Label would take them. Usually just far enough for them to come back for good." (A-Z:93)

Poverty and marginalization are reflected in the town, as these difficult conditions can be seen in the children Jem saw as a rider on the school bus. Abu-Jaber embodies marginalization through children and puts the reader in front of the anxiety she feels about this society in which families cannot properly educate their children.

> "A band of seven children, ranging from around ten to eighteen, emerged from the defunct bus, crossed the lot, and climbed onto the school bus. Jem noticed a

clothesline loaded down with diapers. The Broom kids looked savage. Their faces were sharp and blank, branded with grime. Jem felt heat rising from their hands, their mouths, the way they ran, banging down to sit in the last rows in the bus. (A-Z:91-92)

Arabian Jazz brings us closer to the reality experienced by families in the Euclid area through the Peachy Otts family, which lives next to the Ramoud family, reflecting the life of marginalization and poverty without any horizon. Peachy Otts has two sisters, Glady and Dolores. The latter gave birth to her first child when she was barely twelve.

"she'd turned herself over so many times to that damn man, that damn man being many men, forty, maybe fifty, or even a hundred. Who was counting? It didn't matter, they were all the same, parading around with their dicks like trophies, and nearly every one put a baby in her." (A-Z:101-02)

Through the character of Dolores, Abu-Jaber would like to describe the instability experienced by families in Euclid and their dissatisfaction with themselves, as the role of Dolores became only to get pregnant. While dying, Dolores is still asking about her younger sister, Peachy, as she wants her sister to have a better life than her and go to university to get out of this marginalized place represented by Euclid.

This setting is of paramount importance for the novel. It embodies all the complexity that resides in building the identity of an Arab American family. Euclid is a small copy of the greater American society where Arab Americans struggle to identify themselves. The two sisters will test their strength to overcome this issue in a complex environment.

Diana Abu-Jaber expresses the displacement to which this family of Arab origin is exposed through two important events strongly connected to each other in the novel. The first event is manifested in the family moving from Syracuse to Euclid, and the second event

connected with it is the death of the mother, Nora. Through these two related events, Abu Jaber seeks to highlight the concept of homesickness and the relationship

7

to the mother country.

For Jemorah and Melvina, the loss of their mother is the same as the loss of their home. On the other hand, for Matussem, the event of moving to Euclid is a repetition of the events of his parents' departure from Palestine to Jordan and not returning to the original country again. Thus, Matussem's desire to find a home in Euclid is similar to the desire of his parents to find a home in Jordan.

> *"Euclid, lost to the rest of the world, was Matussem's private land, like the country his parents tried to leave as they made lives in Jordan, as they let go of their children's memories and let them grow up as Jordanians. Matussem was only two when the family left Nazareth. Still he knew there had been a Palestine for his parents; its sky formed a ceiling in his sleep. He dreamed of the country that had been, that he was always returning to in his mind. After they'd moved to Euclid, he found there were ways to lose himself in a place. Euclid, my misplaced past, he thought when he walked the gravel roads, past shacks and barking dogs. When he first saw Euclid he remembered it, every silver leaf and broken-backed creek. Nora had been his history once; now only the land was left." (A-Z:260)*

The mother's loss at an early age made the two girls, Jem and Melvie, experience emotional and psychological displacement, besides the problem of dual identity they suffer from. This situation resulted in a profound impact on the construction of the daughters' identity.

The mother's death, due to typhus during the family's trip to Jordan, cut off the relationship with Nora's parents because the grandparents consider Mattussem to be the cause of their daughter's death and consider the two girls, Jemorah and Melvina, to be accomplices. This made the two girls' isolation worsen, and their relationship with American society further complicated.

Mattussem considers the other half of his two daughters to be Arab, while the grandparents consider him half a criminal, and the two girls have to live with this accusation for the rest of their lives.

> *"His in-laws never forgave him. Although they called the girls on birthdays and holidays, they wouldn't see them in person. "It hurts too much," his mother-in-law had said to Jem, "to see so much of our daughter mixed up with the body of her murderer." (A-Z:85)*

The grandparents' rejection of the Arab half also means stripping the two girls of their American half, judging them as strangers, and placing them in the category of foreigners' subject to hate. Thus, the Ramouds are condemned to be rejected by the family, and the two girls have known this matter since their childhood, as they had an awareness of their difference.

The feeling of difference was increased by the effect of the physical aspect and the skin color, which differs from their peers. The thing that causes them problems often develop into verbal or physical abuse. Jemorah was subjected to this rejection and psychological torture many times on the school bus, and she got off the bus and went straight to her room. It is as if she is escaping to her own world, where no such children exist.

"One day someone tore out a handful of her hair; on another someone pushed her down as she stood to leave; on another someone raked scratches across her face and neck as she stood, her eyes full, the sound of her name ringing in rounds of incantation. Waiting to leave, she could see her name on the mailbox from a half mile away, four inches high in bright red against the black box: RAMOUD. Matussem had been so eager to proclaim their arrival. There was no hiding or disguising it. She would run off the bus, straight to her room, but the voices would follow and circle her bed at night." (A-Z:93)

It is clear that the Arab half of Jemorah, which led to the cut of the relationship with the grandparents, is the same one who caused her trouble with her surroundings.

Abu-Jaber highlights that Jemorah resorts to "invisibility" to confront her painful journey, and "self-erasing" is the only way to escape troubles with her environment. Thus, Arabian *jazz* is a vibrant example of the efforts made by Arab American writers to portray the experience of their suffering within American society and the difficult path they pass through to form their identity.

Another character in the novel was used by Abu Jaber to highlight the racism that Arab Americans and other ethnicities suffer from is Portia. It seems that American society has not yet assimilated the multicultural and ethnic pluralism that constitutes its various components.

The character of Portia, the director of Jemorah at the hospital, was used by

9

Diana Abu Jaber to reflect the arrogant view that white Americans view of other races.

When Jemorah decides to leave her job, she gets a call from Portia in an attempt to keep her under control. Portia's speech was at the height of racism towards Arabs and African Americans. She described Matussem as 'Negro', indicating that the American racist discourse considers 'Negro' everything other than white. Abu-Jaber aims through Portia's speech to reject racist speech in American society as a whole.

> *"Your mother used to be such a good girl. She was so beautifully white, pale as a flower. And then, I don't know. What happened? The silly girl wanted attention. She met your father in her second year [of college] and she just wanted attention... This man, he couldn't speak a word of our language, didn't have a real job. And Nora was so – like a flower, a real flower, I'm telling you. It seemed like three days after she met that man they were getting married. A split second later she was pregnant. I know for a fact her poor mother – your grandmother – had to ask for a picture of the man for her parish priest to show around to prove he wasn't a Negro. Though he might as well have been, really, who could tell the difference, the one lives about the same as the other." (A-Z:293-94)*

In another scene from the novel in which the bias of the whites against Arab Americans appears, Matussem takes his family for a picnic in a park that Abu Jaber called "Fair Haven Park" to give the story a kind of irony.

Matussem served food and drink to two young men in the park and talked for a long time. But the two young men acted strangely when they learned of the Arab origins of the Ramoud family. The behavior of the two young men made Matussem and his family horrified as they packed their luggage and left the park.

> *"that boy made a strange little yelp. "A-rabs!" he said, his eyes now full of what looked like a twist of amusement and disgust. He turned to the other boy and said, "Arabs, Jesus fucking Christ. And we ate their food." The other boy grabbed his friend and tugged him away. As they left, Matussem heard them laughing. No one said much after the boys had gone. They packed up and left soon after. "(A-Z:361)*

As explained and discussed in this axis, Diana Abu-Jaber, in her novel *Arabian Jazz*, depicts the environment in which the events of the novel take place, and how the attitudes of white Americans from different social classes, including the lower classes, are trying to show racial superiority over Arab Americans.

This kind of interaction creates in Arab Americans a form of resistance to overcome discrimination. This leads to strengthening the sense of collective belonging and creates a sense of pride in their identity. Arab Americans also adopt social behaviors that will attenuate rejection.

The difficult situation of this family was aggravated by the absence of the mediation role that the mother Nora played. These Arab American characters find it very difficult to find their way to America. Jem seems to know very well what it means to be an Arab American and is stuck in a situation and a job that she hates. After being shocked by her mother's death, her sister Melvie decides to become a nurse to "fight death", unlike Jemorah, she knows her goals well. Matussem seems lost after the death of his wife and resorts to jazz music as an expression of his desire to integrate the American society.

Abu Jaber wants these characters to struggle to form their identity without the mother, especially the girls Jem and Melvie, whom Abu Jaber leaves to face their own struggles during this journey.

In the midst of this, we find Aunt Fatima, Matussim's sister, trying to fill the gap left by Nora. Abu-Jaber uses her to test the two girls' acceptance of the Arab principles and values that Fatima is trying to pass on to her American nieces.

4- Identity's deconstruction of the main characters

A- Fatima

Diana Abu-Jaber is considered one of the contemporary Arab-American writers who has tackled the issue of identity in a new way. Abu Jaber not only criticized the Americans' racism and anti-Arab behavior, but she also criticized the Arab heritage of the motherland. This criticism of the Arab side required great courage from Abu-Jaber because most writings considered this heritage sacred and not subject to criticism. Abu Jaber critiqued this culture using the character of Fatima.

Aunt Fatima in the novel Arabian Jazz represents the old homeland. She tends to the conservative nature through the values that she wants to preserve in the United States of America. A year after the arrival of Mutassim, her trip to America left behind her difficult circumstances in the country of origin, trauma, death, and poverty. A painful experience

represented mainly in the event of burying four infant sisters with her parents' participation when she was young because of poverty.

> *"When we were homeless and dying without food, what of the four starving babies I had to bury still alive, living —I, I, I?" she said, pushing her palms in their faces, as if the mark of it was there to be read. "Can I buy a bar of American soap and wash these away, as you have washed up yourself? Babies I buried with my mother watching so this rest could live, so my baby brother can eat, so he can move away and never know about it. These why he came here, then," she said, turning to Jem and Melvina. "To get away from knowing. No one would tell, but still he knows there is something to fly from, praise Allah he was born so fortunate! Born a man, not to know the truth." (A-Z: 334)*

The family's sacrifice of some of its members to avoid starvation for others, especially Matussem, was a shock to Fatima, who would pursue her for the rest of her life. Still, this event was also a message to the two sisters to know the social system in the country of origin.

Matussem, the only son of his parents, represents the attention the males receive in the family, while the girls receive insults. This sexual differentiation in the motherland is represented by Aunt Fatima in America. Despite Fatima's awareness of this reality, she defends it and seeks its continuity.

> *"his mother had cradled his head between her breasts, even when he became gangly, arms and legs spilling from her lap. She had stroked his head, called him my eyes, even as she lifted her voice, a shard of anger at his sisters, saying, "Move faster! Awkward, donkey, beanstalk! Lower your face, rude girl!" (A-Z: 187)*

Fatima is the voice of the past in the lives of her nieces, a symbol of preserving values that oppress and devalue women. She believes that a woman's value can only be if she is next to a man. For this reason, she always expresses her concern for the two sisters, Jem and Melvie, and the need to find husbands. Fatima believes that it is her duty to guide the two girls to marriage to preserve the family's honor.

According to Fatima, the husband must be Arab to protect the two sisters from foreign influence and ensure the motherland's continuity in the emigration country. She makes great efforts to build the identity of her nieces and always tries to keep them under her control. Fatima is against mixing with the Americans, to the extent that she wears black at the wedding of a family member who married an American woman as an expression of mourning for the loss of this person.

Fatima's obsession with the traditions and values of the motherland is reflected in her keenness to indoctrinate Jemorah and Melvina that the honor of the family should not be harmed.

> "It seemed to Jem that virtually from the hour of her mother's passing, her aunts had converged around her with warnings about men. They told her: stay with your father, he needs you now; ignore boys, they're stupid and dangerous; you don't know what they can do to you, what they want to do. Each summer, visiting Auntie Nabila or Lutfea or Nejla would take Jem's face between her hands and examine Jem's lips to see if she'd been kissed. "Not yet," they'd whisper, crossing themselves. "Al humad'illah, thanks be to God. She's a good girl!" (A-Z: 9-10)

Abu-Jaber criticizes the widespread image in the Arab countries where women represent the embodiment of family honor and how women's virginity is a symbol of this honor, which makes society exercise control over women's sexuality.

Aunt Fatima then represents an extension of these values and a symbol of their permanence by transmitting these teachings to Jem and Melvie through marriage. According to Fatima, a woman's natural destiny is to marry and have children. The aunt takes advantage of all occasions to search for Arab husbands for the two sisters, and among these occasions is a reception organized by the church in honor of the Archbishop from Jordan.

Fatima built her perceptions about American society through the period she lived there, as she attributes everything that is positive to her homeland and denies the existence of a real American culture worthy of attention. So she refuses to integrate and imposes this on Jem and Melvie. She considers that the danger lies in all that is

American and that Americanization is a danger that threatens the survival of Arab values.

> *"She lived among Americans, in places they had built, among their people, but despite this she wanted to keep herself, her family, and a few friends apart from the rest. She wanted what the Americans had, but at the same time she would never relax her hold on herself. It was not appropriate to mingle. Americans had the money, but Arabs, ah! They had the food, the culture, the etiquette, the ways of being and seeing and understanding how life was meant to be lived. Her wish, always, no matter what, the sharp wish that cut into her center and had lifted her eyes with hope was that her nieces should marry Arab boys, preferably in the family." (A-Z:360)*

B- Matussem

Abu-Jaber uses the father's figure, Matussem, to illustrate the father's influence on how he builds the personality and identity of his daughters. Matussem passed through difficult experiences that formed his character. Losing his motherland, Palestine, living in Jordan, and then emigrating to America and marrying an American woman, the death of his wife, Nora, and the accompanying alienation in the diaspora contributed to building Matussem's personality and his hybrid identity.

Nora's death marked a major turning point in Matussem's life. It was the wife who supported him in America, and she taught him the language of the country. Losing her means losing the link that connects him to America. He understands that Nora's death is one of the important events that changed his life forever. Nora's death made Matussem tend to fill this gap by always gathering memories of his wife.

> *"After her death, the mornings opened in Matussem's bed like gray blossoms, like sharp winged birds slicing dawn in two. Something always reminded him of his loss: seeing the back of his wife's head in a crowd, the flicker of her pale eyes in Jem's dark ones, or Melvina catching her finger to the nape of her neck like her mother." (A-Z: 189-90)*

14

The jazz that Matussem started playing is a haven to compensate for the loss of his wife, and thus jazz plays the role of mediator between him and American society, the same role that his wife played. Thus, jazz music is a memory of his lost wife.

These difficult circumstances that Matussem lives in did not affect his role as a father in raising his two daughters.

Matussem makes stories to transmit Arab culture to his daughters, and in his stories, he mixes childhood memories with fairy tales. He aims, through these stories, to keep an Arab memory alive in his daughters and thus build the Arab part of the identity of Melvina and Jemorah.

Matussem uses the characters of the stories he tells in his surroundings, where he calls each person he knows the name of a character from his tales. According to Matussem, this must help him understand the people around him and ease American society's tension and complexity.

Matussem's relationship with Jordan is complicated. Despite his love for his country, he does not want to live in it, nor does he want his daughters to stay in Jordan. Matussem does not want his daughters to live under the social restrictions that dominate society in his homeland. Despite the difficulty of living in America, he prefers that his daughters form their dual identity in this country.

It seems that Matussem is not the embodiment of the strict conservative Arab father; on the contrary, he is open and understanding, and this is due to the experiences he accumulated in both cultures.

Matussem represents the father close to his daughters, the understanding father who always stands in the face of his sister Fatima and prevents her from affecting his daughters, and rejects her point of view and her obsession with finding Arab husbands. He himself married Noora out of love, he *"would never throw them into unwanted marriage." (A-Z: 178)*

For Matussem, it is important not to force his daughters to follow Arab traditions because what interests him is their happiness. The father's role here is crucial in letting his daughters benefit from freedom in the country and build their hybrid identity in this environment. Matussem does this because he believes in the need to integrate into American society, just as he employs jazz music for the same purpose.

C- The two daughters

Jemorah and Melvina lived a life full of contradictions that made forming their dual identities a complex task.

The contradictions began with the event of Aunt Fatima's visit to Matussem's family immediately before traveling to Jordan, where Jemorah was nine years old. The aunt spoke to her, assuring her that they would return home, marry a lovely Arab, and have children. Fatima considers that the home of her nieces is Jordan and insists that the two girls are Arabs. These words disturbed Nora, the American mother, who adopts a different perception, and she commented on Fatima's sayings:

> "Nora's lips tightened to a streak. She stood and left the room... Later at night, Nora bent over the girls, tucking them in. "Your home is here. Oh, you will travel, I want you to. But you always know where your home is." The ends of her straight, long hair brushed their faces, its bright red fringes swinging and making sparks. Soon they would be flying to the moon to visit their other family." (A-Z: 78)

Nora wants the two girls to know about their father's country, but she considers them Americans, and they should not forget that.

During this trip, the two girls became familiarized with the difference between the two cultures through the conflict between Nora and Matussem's sisters. In this way, from an early age, the two girls witnessed the difference between the two cultures to the point of conflict. And this creates for them a contradiction in self-definition and the duality of identity.

The death of the mother complicates this process, and this is what produced the two opposing personalities of the two sisters. Jemorah, twenty-nine years old, a dreamer who lacks self-confidence, and twenty-two-year-old Melvina, the realistic girl.

Melvina decided to become a nurse after discovering her inability at the moment of her mother's death. She was unable to help her avoid her fate. This painful experience drove her to prove her identity and dedicate the rest of her life to the nursing profession and saving people's lives. Her devotion to her work also made her devoted to serving and caring for her family members.

> "The day before she'd given her father diet cards with long lists of foods he was not, under any circumstances, to touch. She'd also given him a paramedic's first-aid kit, full of things like surgical thread and booster shots for malaria, hepatitis, and typhus – especially typhus." (A-Z: 265)

Devotion to work for Melvina is the way to impose her personality and prove herself in American society; she is the main nurse in the hospital, although she is twenty-two years old.

> "The staff in her hospital and the hospital community at large knew and respected her and honored her commands. Doctors consulted her as a matter of course. Patients and their families sent her flowers, chocolates, even jewelry – which she promptly returned, not wishing to appear compromised." (A-Z:179)

Melvina's rational personality taught her how to build her identity at an equal distance from the Arab and American cultures. She helps her sister Jemorah make difficult decisions, urging her not to give any importance to their aunt's obsession. Melvina often resists her Aunt Fatima's attempts to rebuild the social reality of the motherland. It criticizes the Arab culture when necessary and seeks to reconcile the two cultures.

> "Excuse me, but what were you saying just now?" Melvie asked Fatima, fists on her hips. Estrelia tried to wave Melvie away, but the confrontation thrilled Fatima; gin was boiling through her, mingling with a hundred grievances and irritations. Zaeed was up on the dance floor with Amy; there was nothing to constrain Fatima; she was free. Soaring on a hot wind of anger, she shouted, "Your mother dies on because she hates Arabs!" Melvina slapped her so hard that Fatima spilled out of her chair." (A-Z:66)

Despite these behaviors from Melvina, which seems at first glance not to respect Arab traditions, especially respect for the elderly, the reality is that she has all the respect and appreciation for her Arab part and her Arab background. This situation makes her more reconciled with herself and her heritage; she respects her Arab belonging but reserves the right to criticize it when necessary.

Melvina celebrates her Americanness through her loyalty to her work, an essential part of her life, and her cultural and emotional independence and freedom. On the other hand, she celebrates her Arabness by being proud of her Arab part and recognizing it as an important component of her identity.

Jemorah is completely different from her sister Melvina. While Melvina knows what she wants, Jemorah is subject to a complex struggle to construct her dual identity. Her uncertainty in the issue of her identity made her oscillate between the Arab part and the American part of her culture. From the novel's beginning, it becomes clear that Jemorah does not make an effort to move forward in her life. The same hospital where the sister's work represents "life" for Melvina, but it is a large prison for Jemorah.

Jemorah lives a huge gap in her life, trying to fill it with childhood memories with her mother, Nora. Thus, remaining in her place without progress prevents her from defining her identity and building her personality.

The calamity of her mother's death came as a great shock; she was nine years old when she witnessed the death scene. Her shock made her live the pain in silence, forming a world of her own to escape reality and ease this suffering.

The stories that Mutassim used to tell his daughters made Jemorah merge with the characters of these stories and use them, as Mutassim does, in real life; this makes her personality dreamy and unrealistic.

This uncertain state of Jemora made her not accomplish several works she had started. Hesitation is her life companion, confirming her deep duplicity, negativity, and failure.

> *"I'm tired to fight it out here. I don't have much idea of what it is to be Arab, but that's what the family is always saying we are. I want to know what part of me is Arab. I haven't figured out what part is our mother, either. It's like she abandoned us, left us alone to work it all out." (A-Z:307-08)*

Jemorah suffers from the death of her mother, who was her connection to American society. But she wants to end her suffering and find balance in her both cultural parts. She decides to leave her inner world into the real world. And the first step she took was to give up her job at the hospital, which she always hated, and decided to move to California to complete her university studies.

This decision made her start a new stage in building her hybrid identity, allowing her to enjoy the diversity that characterizes her culture.

It is clear that Diana Abu Jaber's novel *Arabian Jazz* makes how to build a hybrid identity among Arab Americans the focus of her discourse. She confirms that this identity's construction passes through many complex stages and is embodied through continuous communication with the self.

5- Conclusion

In this paper, I dealt with the approach of the concept of identity among contemporary Arab American writers through the novel of Diana Abu Jaber, *Arabian Jazz.*

I devoted to trace the development of Arab American literature through the Arab presence in the United States of America for more than a century. And we found that the writings of each stage reflect the history and conditions of the society and the efforts of its members to prove themselves as part of the American society.

Also I dealt with an analysis of Diana Abu Jaber's novel *Arabian jazz* in which I analyze the general context of the novel and its connection to the concept of identity building among Arab Americans by deconstructing the identity aspect of the main characters in the novel. The difference that characterizes these characters in their perception of the concept of identity and how each one of them builds it.

This paper shows that Arab American writers have great maturity in dealing with the issue of identity in the context of a multicultural American society, mainly due to their extensive knowledge of the American society in which they live and their pride in their Arab heritage. This situation made them defend their Arab part, criticizing it if necessary and trying to change the stereotyped images of Arabs without preventing them from establishing their sense of belonging to American society. Thus, the balance between cultural components is their discourse's basis.

Arabian Jazz by Diana Abu-Jaber is a fitting example of how contemporary Arab American writers have approached the concept of identity by focusing on both cultural components of Arab Americans.

The main characters in the novel knew how to build their hybrid identity after an internal struggle and a complex path. The two sisters, Jemorah and Melvina, in an environment with two languages, two cultures, and two families, faced this difficult task with much patience and perseverance, with the help of Father Matussem, who guaranteed them freedom of choice. Though Aunt Fatima's attempts to influence the two sisters and her obsession with reproducing the culture of the mother country in the diaspora.

The novel uses jazz as a metaphor through which Matussem attempts to alleviate the racism that Arabs are subjected to and comfort himself with it from loss and displacement. Jazz also indicates a common ground between Arab and American cultures.

6- Bibliography

Abu-Jaber, Diana. *Arabian Jazz*. 1993

Majaj, Lisa Suhair."New Directions: Arab American Writing at Century's End." Post
Gibran: Anthology of New Arab American Writing. New York: Syracuse UP, 1999

Naff, Alixa. "Arabs in America: A Historical Overview." Arabs in the New
World: Studies on Arab-American Communities. Ed. Sameer Y. Abraham and
Nabeel Abraham. Detroit: Wayne State University, 1983

Salaita, Steven."Split Vision: Arab /American Literary Criticism." *Al-Jadid* 6.32.
(Summer 2000)

Salaita, Steven. "Sand Niggers, Small Shops, and Uncle Sam: Cultural
Negotiation in the Fiction of Joseph Geha and Diana Abu-Jaber." Criticism 43.4
(Fall 2001)

Shakir, Evelyn."Arab American Literature." *New Immigrant Literatures in
the United States: A Source Book to Our Multicultural Literary Heritage*. Ed. Alpana
Sharma Knippling. Westport: Greenwood Publishing, 1996

Suleiman, Michael. Early Arab-Americans: The Search for Identity.

Suleiman, Michael. "Introduction." Arabs in America: Building a New
Future. Ed. Suleiman. Philadelphia: Temple UP, 1999